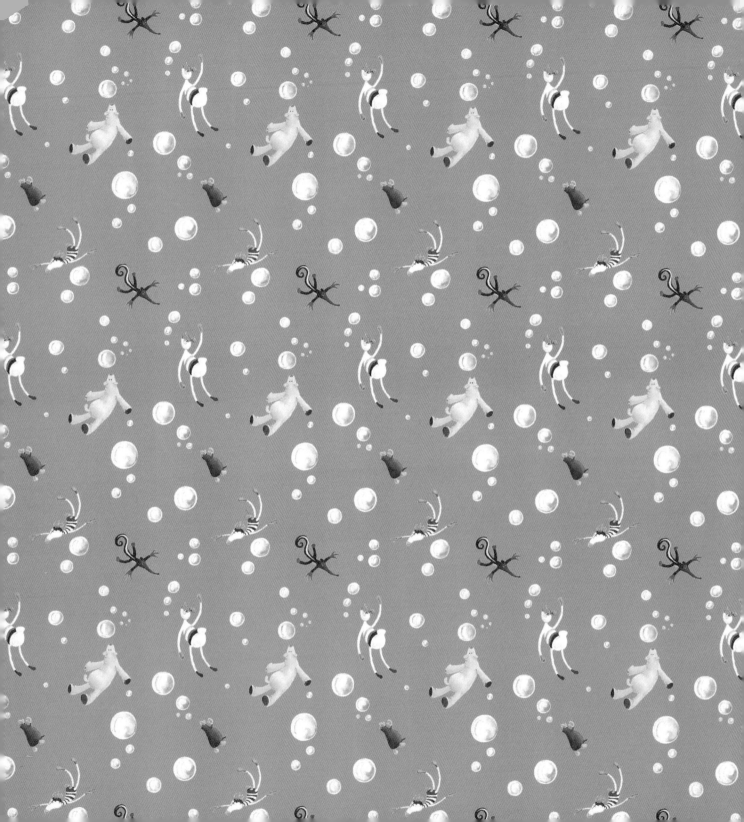

Imagine a planet, somewhere in a distant galaxy,
made entirely out of soap and bubbles;
Planet O'Sudds.
Living on that planet are the friendliest, funniest
and fuzziest aliens you could ever meet; the Filzkins.
Follow their adventures as they embark on a
dangerous rescue mission into outer space in their
newly invented spacebubbleship.
Fasten your seatbelt and prepare for a bumpy ride.

The adventure has just begun…

ISBN 978-1-9999506-0-6

Text, Illustration and Colouring of the Illustrations are

Copyright © 2017 of Rhian and Ingo Hans of Sebold's originals

www.seboldsoriginals.com

Sebold's originals

We would like to thank all of you
who have supported us over the years, from those
of you who have a favourite Filzkin living at home with you,
to those of you who simply love them all.
This book exists because of you.

A special thank you to Noriko & Taro Yoshioka,
Bernd Altmann and Clemens Altmann.

A very special thank you to Liz Edney,
for helping to blump out this "bubble".

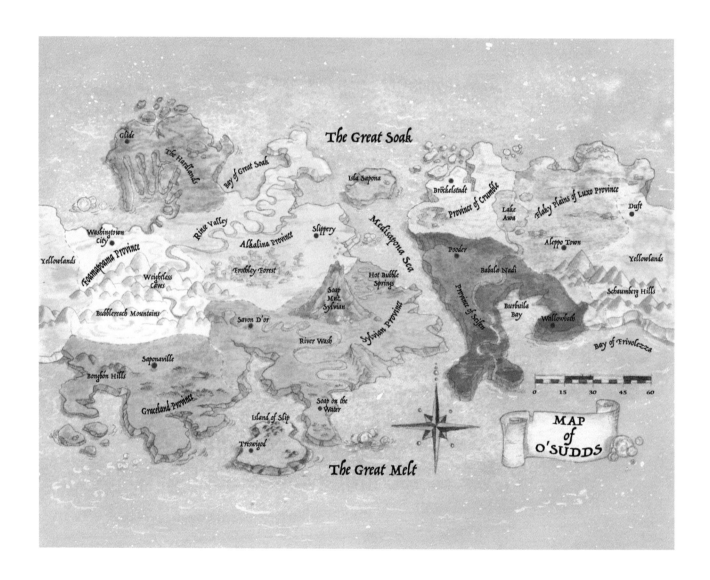

Rhian & Ingo Hans

The
FILZKINS®
Take Off

The Wooliest Aliens
In The Universe

CONTENTS

CHAPTER 1

Bubblefall

Mr. McKarr felt the first bubbles of the season with his finger tip. "Ahh…" he said to himself as he wiped a voluminous bubble away from his nose, "it's that wonderful time of year again."

O'Sudds was a planet made, entirely, of soap, so there were always a lot of bubbles to be seen, but this was Bubblefall which meant that there would be even more than usual. The Filzkins, loved bubbles of all kinds and Mr. McKarr was no different.

It all started a long, long time ago. Far out in the universe, where one would expect nothing to exist at all, there were a few vital elements floating around. H_2O, better known as water, BBF_1 (fluff) and $C_{17}H_{35}COONa$ (soapy flakes). The incredible force of atmospheric turbulence, worked rather like a tumble dryer, mixing these three elements together creating this wonderful soapy planet.

In the great darkness of the cosmos, the tumbling woolly fluff mixed with the compounds of soapy water particles, causing an enormous colour festival! It must have been a magnificent sight.

This planet, offered the perfect conditions for the birth of a new life form, the Filzkins. The Filzkins are made mainly of fluff that had floated away, unnoticed, over many thousands of milworth, from other planets including our very own Planet Earth.

The early ancestors probably named their planet O'Sudds because of the vast, deep oceans of bubbles and soapy water that sloshed about there.

Made of soft woolly fluff and air, the Filzkins are gentle and lighthearted beings. They are inquisitive and have some rather peculiar habits.

As Mr. McKarr sniffed the air with his long nose, he couldn't help but think about his old friend, Edgar. He missed him and wished they were spending Bubblefall together.

He remembered the fun-filled evenings they had spent last Fluffdown, talking about travelling into outer space. He loved to hear the tales that Edgar told about his grandmother, Cornice Thellwell. She had been a famous space traveller. She had made several spectacular journeys strapped to the back of a bubble.

It had always been Edgar's dream to follow in her footsteps. And not long ago, Edgar had set off on a voyage of his own in his specially designed "one-Filzkin" capsule.

Mr McKarr had not been at all happy when he saw that his friend would only have a small bubble-pod to protect him. He had tried to persuade him to wait until Doc.Hibbert's Spacebubbleship was ready when they could all travel safely together.

However, Edgar was set on going it alone. Now, he had not returned and nobody had heard from him for ollards.

Was he lost in space, just floating around all alone and probably rather hungry by now? Or had he landed on another planet and perhaps met other beings? Were they friendly? Or not, he wondered.

Mr. McKarr was kind and well-meaning, if a little bossy at times. He liked to get his yellow nose-tip into everything.

He never doubted his own abilities and truly believed he could do absolutely anything. He felt it to be his duty to help any Filzkin in need, and he was sure that Edgar was in need now.

He made a decision there and then to go and find Edgar. He would do whatever it took to bring him back. There was no time to waste.

Back in his home, Mr. McKarr went straight to his bubblestream.

(A bubblestream is similar to our telephone. It has a complex network of underground pipes transporting tiny sonic bubbles through a thick soapy liquid). Mr. McKarr spoke loudly into the mouthpiece.

"Hello, hello … Is that The Space Science and Out of This World Research Department…?

Could I please speak to Professor Doctor Hibbert?"
A gurgle spurted out from the depths of the bell jar as a bubble popped its message,

"Hello, DocHibbert speaking."

"Hello Doc, this is Mr. McKarr!" gurgle and plop!

"Ahh, Mr. McKarr, any news of Edgar?"

"...that's what I wanted to talk to you about … can I come over, today?"

CHAPTER 2

The Slurch

That afternoon Mr. McKarr got ready to go and see Doc Hibbert at his laboratory in Washingtown City. Doc Hibbert was the top space scientist on O'Sudds, he led a team of space-geek-Filzkins that included Mr. McKarr and Edgar. At the moment he was busy building a bubbleship to take into outer space to explore worlds where no Filzkin had gone before.

After tying a black & white neckerchief around his neck and popping on his gloves, Mr. McKarr left his house and set off along the slippery path.

At the top of the hill a few slurches were bobbing on their hover stations as usual. Powered by micro magnetic waves from deep underground, slurches are individual capsules. They drift around unattended in towns and cities all over O'Sudds and provide free transport for everyone.

"Oh Wow!" exclaimed Mr McKarr, "OH WOW! AWESOME!"

He had spotted a gleaming new slurch in a two-tone crimson and turquoise combo, it was one of the latest models too, an xQ 20 Pod-Pod. He was smitten! Prone to crazes Mr. McKarr always got excited about new gadgets.

He quickly clambered in to the slurch. Once securely strapped in to his seat, he pressed the start button and surged forward, heading towards Washingtown City. He was so excited by the extra power in this new model, that he didn't notice the froth and fizz he was leaving behind. Any passers by would have been blown off their feet in the clouds of bubbles that his speeding was creating.

Marvelling at the falling bubbles bursting on his windscreen, he swerved and whizzed his way through the high-rise soap towers and multi-coloured buildings of Saponaville.

He could see over the roofs of houses and in through the windows of the towers. He always enjoyed this birds-eye view of his hometown and being a nosey-parker, loved to see what his neighbours were up to.

In the distance he could see the craggy hills of the Bubble reach Mountains. Beyond these hills was the crater of Foamapoama where Washingtown City was nestling.

Because it was Bubblefall, the air was alive with bubbles. They were floating gently or jetting vertically out of holes in the ground. There were all kinds of bubbles, from tiny, almost invisible bubbles to giant, floppy bubbles. Occasionally, there were geysers of hot steaming bubbles shooting up into the sky.

It was so much fun driving the slurch that he couldn't resist pushing it to its limits so he pulled sharply on the seismic propeller lever. Suddenly, he was skimming over bumps and sailing down inclines at at least 150 ronalds per allor. Once, he zoomed up a hill with such force that he soared over the top and flew straight into an unexpected geyser. This gave him quite a start. For a moment his stomach was in his throat and his heart nearly stopped beating.

He had lost control. Propelled upwards in the gush of hot vapours and suds, his ears popped and his claw hands leapt off the steering wheel as if it was red hot. He found himself on the fountain top of the geyser bouncing around like a ping-pong ball. He was helpless!

As luck would have it, the xQ 20 Pod-Pod happened to have a built in anti-geyser-trapping button, which was turbo driven with a rev-reducing system to boot. He pressed the button as hard as he could. There was a sudden boost of power and a shift of gear, taking him out of danger and swooping him down to a safer level. "Phew! Frothy suds! That was close." he exclaimed. Whistling, as if

nothing had happened, Mr. McKarr looked around to see if anyone had seen his reckless driving. Thankfully there was no one in sight.

He thought of Edgar out in space and wondered if he'd had any similar hairy moments.

Soon the bowl shaped crater of Washingtown City appeared in front of him, he was nearly there.

Would the Bubbleship be ready, he wondered?

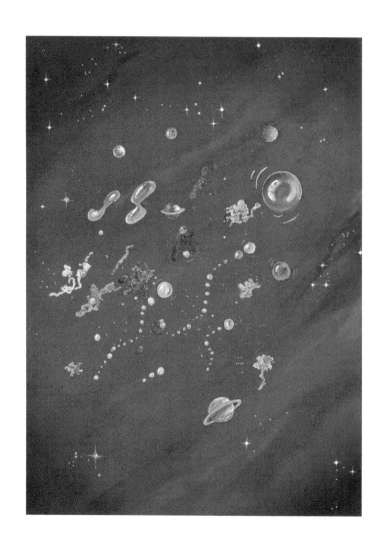

CHAPTER 3

Lost in Space

Somewhere out in space, Edgar was hovering happily along in his capsule.

In order to launch it, he had had to climb all the way up to the top of Soap Mount Sylvian, pulling the "bubble-pod" behind him. Once at the top he climbed into his ship and allowed the high winds to carry him away.

He was lifted off with some force, upwards into the sky. At first his journey was very bumpy as he passed through the thick clouds of bubbles that blocked his way, but once he had left the atmosphere of O'Sudds, his capsule cruised along steadily.

He was amazed by what he saw. The Universe truly was, astounding! Just as his grandma Cornice had described. In front of him was a never ending sky of pink and purple. Soap flakes tumbled around him and bubbles of all kinds glinted in the light of the moon. There were single bubbles and sometimes strings of bubbles and clusters of bouncing bubbles. Amongst them, he spotted a few squiggles of rolling tumble-fluff.
Edgar thoroughly enjoyed his first few allors bobbing gently along in his pod.

He felt very proud to be following in his Granny's footsteps, venturing out into space on his own.

During this time he managed to collect a lot of different samples of bubbles, some solar soap and some very rare cosmic flakes. However, fluff was his special interest, and unfortunately this was proving hard to find. He was slightly puzzled, he had expected much more of it to be around.

He was soon to find out why this was.

There was a cosmic storm brewing!

He could see it in the distance, like a dark, purple bruise on the sky way ahead of him. At first it seemed quite a long way away but in no time at all, Edgar found himself in the eye of the storm.

An enormous cosmic rumble had gathered all the floating fluff and woolly particles into a great swirling mass. He had never seen anything like it, so much fluff! He was quite excited at first and would have loved to have taken some samples, but that was out of the question. A lot of it had formed into balls, some as big as his own space pod!

Any excitement he had soon disappeared, as he desperately tried to manoeuvre his capsule between the swarming balls. There were so many of them! It was impossible to dodge them all, as they flew at high speed towards him. He was continuously buffeted about, as his pod was hit from all directions. It was a real struggle to keep the pod under control as he was thrown from side to side inside it. He really wondered how much more his bubble-pod could take.

The sticky surface of his bubble-pod was now rapidly becoming coated in fluff until finally he couldn't see out at all!

He was trapped inside a rolling and ever growing, fluff-ball, being tossed about like a rag doll!

On and on and ON it went!

After what seemed like forever, the storm began to die down. By this time his capsule had gathered so much fluff that it had more than doubled in size!

With all the tumbling in the storm, the fluff had felted, binding him inside unable to see out.

Poor Edgar! He had no idea just how thick the layer of fluff surrounding him had become.

Things were not looking too good for him *inside* his pod either. His solar powered light needed the sun's rays and these were now being blocked out.

He would have to think fast, because soon he would be in total darkness with no idea where he was going!

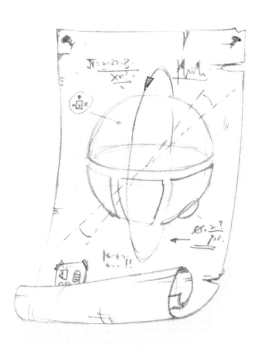

CHAPTER 4

The Spacebubbleship

Mr. McKarr was astounded by what he saw when he entered Doc Hibbert's laboratory. Hovering in front of him was the almost completed spacebubbleship. Tethered by ropes to stop it from floating away, the transparent sphere, with its coat of swirling colours, quivered gently in the light. Through its iridescent bubble wall, Mr. McKarr could see all sorts of paraphernalia. It thrilled him to think that this was the biggest spacebubbleship ever created and, that soon, they would be floating away in it.

Doc Hibbert was concentrating hard on a wall covered in complicated drawings.

From beneath the Bubbleship, Arthur's curling tail could be seen.

Arthur, Doc Hibbert's assistant, was good at making things out of nothing, a skill that Doc Hibbert found very useful in the laboratory.

Arthur reached out for a nearby soap-grip tool, Mr. McKarr, trying to help as usual, leaned over to pass it to him. As he did so he tripped over one of the ropes holding down the spacebubbleship. This caused it to wobble out of position and float upwards into the air, bouncing like a hollow jelly.

Poor Arthur was lifted up with the bubbleship and dangled there wondering for a second what had happened. Doc Hibbert came to his rescue along with Mr. McKarr but Arthur wasn't too keen on any more of Mr. McKarr's help.

"Well, what do you think?" asked Doc Hibbert, looking proudly at his creation.

"It's beautiful," Mr. McKarr replied, "it's amazing … it's … it's, it's a bubble! And a spaceship! It really is a space-bubble-ship! But tell me how can a bubble go into space? Won't it just burst?"

"Aaah, well, you see," he replied "the spacebubbleship is no ordinary bubble! I designed it to withstand the changes in air pressure in deepest space" he explained.

"It's made of an extra strong soapy membrane and should safely travel through space at an average speed of 37.6 tickles per allor. It's completely safe, unless of course any sharp meteor particles should hit it. But there's nothing we can do about that!"

"What would happen then?" asked Mr. McKarr.

Doc Hibbert responded by making a loud "Pop" with his paw in his cheek.

Ignoring this worrying thought, Mr. McKarr went on "So when can we go Doc? Edgar, may be in terrible trouble we need to go as soon as we can!"

"We are far from ready, my dear fellow." replied Doc, looking over his glasses, "we have a lot more work to do. We haven't even tested our newly developed bubble-heads on the crew yet!"

At that moment Arthur scurried over, wiping suds from his long fluffy claws and generally looking very pleased with himself.

"Well, Doc, I think we could do it! I've just fitted you up with a glycerine equalizer, and it looks pretty good," he said. "It's not quite the one I wanted, but I think it could do for this trip. I could try and get a two-ply double gravity equalizer, but that will take a little more time, of course!"

"It's too risky Arthur, really … and besides, the crew won't be ready yet," Doc insisted.

"But, we've *got* to get going as soon as we can if we're going to find Edgar alive!" said Mr. McKarr.

"Do you think you could have it ready in 5 whortles time?" he continued. "I can gather the crew by then.

 What do you think Arthur?"

"Let's talk about it over a nice cup of tea," said Doc.

They continued their discussion while drinking Sapona Bush tea and eating whirtleberry pie with soda cream.

As the tea frothed wonderfully over Mr. McKarr's lips he couldn't help thinking that Doc Hibbert had even made a science out of making tea!

By the end of their break, they all agreed that this trip should happen, and as soon as possible. So, leaving Doc Hibbert and Arthur to finish their work, Mr. McKarr set off to gather the rest of the crew.

Meanwhile, unbeknown to them, a little blue Filzkin named Boris, had been listening to their every word through the open window.

That evening back in his house Mr.McKarr felt very pleased. He had spent the afternoon bubble-streaming each of the crew members.

They'd arranged to meet the following day, at the Weightless Caves, to test out their bubble helmets before going into deep space.

He fell asleep that night dreaming that he was hurtling, uncontrollably, through the universe in the two-tone slurch.

CHAPTER 5

Bubble-heads

The next day Mr. McKarr and all the crew met at the entrance to the Weightless Caves. The atmosphere here, was perfect for testing the bubble-heads. The bubble helmets would be needed to allow them to survive if they were to find themselves outside the spaceship.

However, they weren't as easy to use as they looked! Each of the crew struggled with them in different ways.

Moley, being small, found that his bubble helmet was so large that he fitted completely inside of it. He found himself having to run continuously on the spot to stop himself from turning upside-down.

"*You* can laugh Enoch, look at yourthelf!" said Moley with his lisp from inside his bubble cage, "Why don't we thwap!" It was true, Enoch couldn't get off the ground as his bubble head was so small that it barely covered his snout!

"I can't stop spinning!" called Nevin in a panic from inside his bubble-head. He was using one spoon hand to paddle himself forward, but found himself spinning around uncontrollably until he was quite dizzy. "Use both hands!" they all shouted together. This made poor Nevin blush, he hand't thought of that.

Reaching to help Hyssop with his bubble-head, Mr. McKarr forgot how soft and gluey, the helmets were. And before they knew it, their bubble-heads stuck together with a loud sticky clap.

As other Filzkins tried to pull them apart they also got stuck!

This made Pink Dawg laugh so hard inside his bubble-head that the bauble on the end of his tail began to swing from side to side like a pendulum. The more he barked the more he swung. Finally after a lot of laughter they managed to free themselves. As they got the hang of wearing them they really began to enjoy the feeling of floating freely, and could now start to imagine themselves in outer space.

From his hiding place, Boris watched in amazement as they moved silently and elegantly in the glistening, blue, depths of the cave. It was like watching a slow-motion water ballet.

Later, when their training was finished they stumbled out under the evening sky. They were a little wobbly on their feet, after the weightlessness of the cave but what fun they had had!

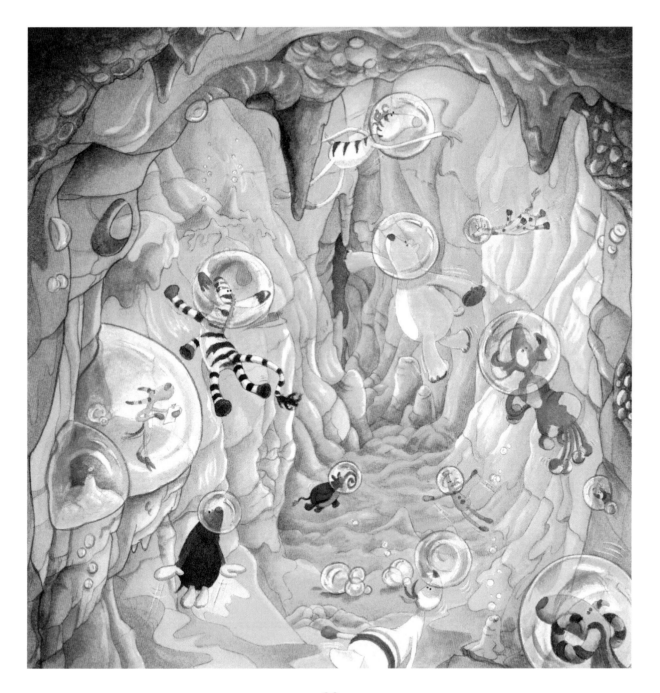

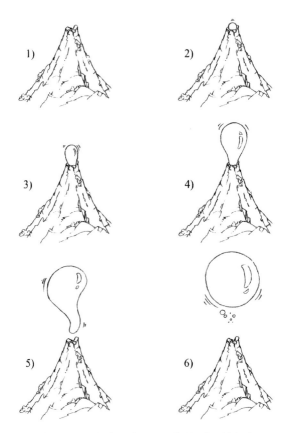

1)

2)

3)

4)

5)

6)

Diagram of the phases of the Bubblerise

CHAPTER 6

Soap Mount Sylvian

What a sky it was that evening, clear and bright with the twin suns going down behind Soap Mount Sylvian on the horizon.

Soap Sylvian is the largest "soapcano" on the planet. "Soapcanoes", are like the volcanoes on Earth, but are made of soap. This one is 1,300 padolitors high! When it erupts spectacular fountains of froth gush up into the sky and hundreds of barolitors of hot suds pour down the sides of the mountain, creating great slippery slopes.

Enoch walked towards Soap Sylvian with Mr. McKarr on one side and Hyssop on the other. Moley had hitched a ride on the end of his trunk and Nevin held on to his tail.

"Oh look!" said Enoch, "there's a "bubblerise" just starting. What perfect timing!"

A "bubblerise" happens when the largest bubble on the planet is let off from the top of the mountain.

They were all very excited.

A chance to see the bubble swelling on the peak in the distance was too irresistible to miss.

Together they waited…

A clear oozing bulge began to emerge and take shape on the summit. The double glint cast upon it by the twin suns, made it shine brilliantly. A most beautiful dome was forming, its skin aswirl with every colour in the rainbow. The Filzkins were spellbound.

As it grew larger and fuller it was pulled dangerously out of shape by the wind high on the summit. But, still it would not let go. The resplendent air ball held on to its birth place, as if afraid to be set free, its glossy film undulating gently in the pink of the evening light.

It would have to fly soon or it would surely burst!

The tension grew. They all knew that it meant bad luck, if a rising bubble burst before leaving the summit. But if it survived, and then flew away, that would bring good luck to all those who saw it.

Awestruck they stared, mouths gaping and tails wagging, until, with a sudden gust of wind and a loud "PING...NG...NG...NG!!" which echoed across the valley, the great bubble was unleashed.

Now, a beautiful and perfect sphere, the super-bubble bounced once, as if to correct itself, and then blithely wobbled off on the breeze.

Soon, it had floated off into the distance, merrily in search of a life of it's own, perhaps in some distant galaxy.

Pablo very rarely spoke but when he did he spoke wisely. Now was one of those moments. "The gift of a bubble-*rise* should be seen as a special *prize*." he said simply.

Even Nevin, always such a worrier, looked happier. There were cheers and jumps for joy and feelings of relief, as they thought of their challenging mission ahead.

"Let's have a party!" said Nielson "I can't think of a better reason to celebrate!"

Not that Nielson ever needed a reason to celebrate "we might not see another one for a while."

"Yes," said Mr. McKarr "Beetroot, your place isn't far from here, let's go there, what do you think?" and before Beetroot had a chance to answer, he continued "excellent, that's settled then, let's go!"

As the twin suns gave way to the "Motherlight" (the large Moon of O'Sudds) they noisily set off to Beetroot's home.

No one noticed the little blue figure rolling along behind them, muttering to himself "Party? Did they say party?"

CHAPTER 7

The Pan-Kalang

Beetroot's home was in effect an elaborate tree house, which overhung the riverbank.

Being a passionate music lover, Beetroot owned a Pan-Kalang. The others knew this. They had played on it many times and couldn't wait to play it again!

The Pan-Kalang is a very strange looking instrument. There is something for everyone in the Pan-Kalang. For the stomper, there is a large foot pump and pedals. For the strummer, there are strings. For the clanger, there are sheets of tin plates to clang and for those who like to use their lungs and blow, there are tubes and pipes of a great variety. The whole construction works like a giant concertina that lifts up and down giving out the constant whir of a smooth horn sound. Coming out of it's centre is a large glass ball, half full of gloopy liquid that makes noisy gurgling sounds as bubbles rise through it. There are antennae with giant beans on their ends, that when pulled, make a hollow "ba-boing" sound as they bounce.

The Pan-Kalang can make so many different sounds! It can clap, ting and whistle. It can toot, ring and grizzle. It can ping, boing and pootle.

It can make a wah, rattle, hoot, and howl. And it can swiffer and swazzle. So it's no surprise that the Filzkins love it so much.

Each Filzkin quickly found his favourite part of the instrument and began to play. And what a din they made. If truth be told, and I think it should be, for us Earthlings it would have been very hard to tell whether they were actually playing a tune or not, so different was it from our music.

They played with joy; some wobbling their heads rhythmically to a strange and irregular beat, others moving an arm or a leg outwards or up into the air, sometimes leaving the instrument, to dance themselves into a dreamy trance. It was clear to see that, for the Filzkins, this was music and they loved it.

As they danced and played, little blue Boris with his restless legs looked on with envy until he could resist no longer. He crept out of his hiding place and sidled up to the edge of the circle. Try as he could he was only Filzkin and could not stop himself.

Slowly at first, but gradually faster and faster and more and more wildly, he began to dance along to the music.

Sometimes he jumped high up into the air. His spring was so powerful, he could bounce as high as the bubble clouds, falling back down to bounce just as high again. Sometimes he would stay afloat in the air a little bit longer, adding little tricks and turns while he was up there. His exotic aerial pranks infuriated Hyssop who believed himself to be the best dancer on O'Sudds. Determined not to be outshone by the gatecrasher, Hyssop too started to perform elaborate pirouettes.

They continued to play and dance on long after midnight, hardly noticing the twin suns rise again, turning their night into day.

Unnoticed, Boris crept quietly down into a hole in the ground.

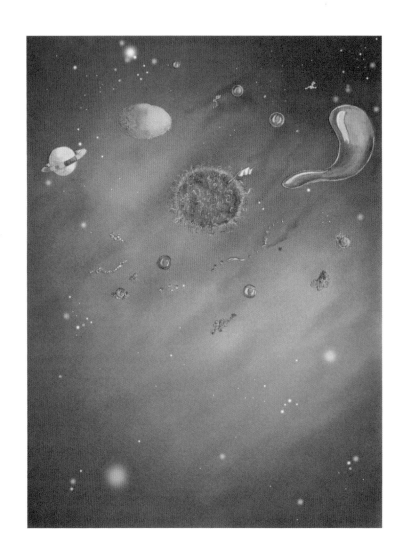

CHAPTER 8

Up Fluff-Creek

Meanwhile, out in space, floating between an egg shaped moon and a strange morphing bubble, was a large ball of fluff. No one would have ever guessed, that hidden deep inside it was Edgar's little space capsule. It could easily have been mistaken for a small planet with a white flag fluttering about on it.

Edgar had managed with great effort to pierce a hole through the thick woolly coat that now encased his bubble-pod, and through it, had poked a white hankie, in the hope that someone might see it and come to his rescue.

By now he was in complete darkness inside his capsule and he was having to feel around for everything. He was surprised that he wasn't in more of a panic. He was worried, yes, but he was still able to think clearly and remember all the things that he had been taught about surviving a space catastrophe.

The one thing that he was certain of, was, that he had to get out of his woolly prison somehow.

If he were out in the open, he thought, he could try space paddling somewhere or he might perhaps be spotted by a passer by.

So began the long, slow process of cutting himself out of his pod.

It seemed to take forever, but at long last, he popped his head out of his woollen cocoon. There couldn't have been a more peculiar sight, even with all the strangeness of outer space. Emerging with his bulbous bubble-head and moving very slowly, Edgar looked like a weird insect or an alien chick hatching from an egg.

Finally, after a long struggle, he was free and floating.

Looking back, and seeing the size of the fluff ball that his capsule had turned into, he was very impressed. After searching for so long for space fluff samples now he had way more than he could handle. But sadly, fluff would be of no use to him now!

Suddenly poor Edgar felt very sorry for himself, as he found himself space paddling in outer space without a paddle.

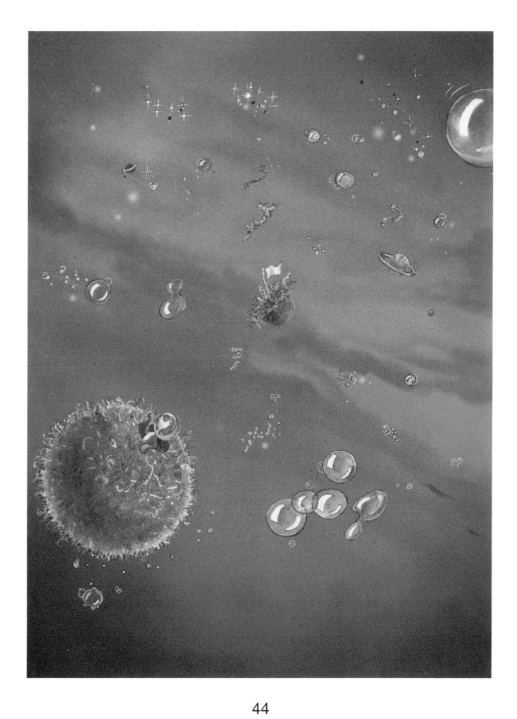

CHAPTER 9

Hot Bubble-Springs

Back on O'Sudds the Filzkins were splashing around happily in a hot bubble-spring. Swishing and sploshing around in the suds, they were all soon smothered in lather. The happiest of them all was Nielson, he was the one who most enjoyed wallowing in sudsy water. He even had his very own tub at home.

They were talking about the large bubble Mount Sylvian had set free for their good fortune.

"I've never seen anything like it! It was simply sublime!" said Muli, dreamily, while styling his wet mane into shape.

"Ahhhh, it was frankly unforgetta-bubble!" said Nielson and they all giggled.

"Do you think we'll see it up there when we fly?" Nevin asked.

"Don't be silly, Nevin, bubbles can't survive in outer space! They would pop just like the ones in this bath," said Nielson, casually blowing a large bubble from the tip of his nose and popping it with his soft hoof.

"…Erm, so what about the space-*bubble*-ship, that we will be travelling in?" asked Nevin nervously.

There was an uncomfortable silence until Mr. McKarr said "no need to worry about that, Doc Hibbert has designed our spacebubbleship with a highly fortified bubble membrane, capable of withstanding the changes in air pressure in deep space!" he said repeating Doc, word for word.

Then quickly changing the subject, he asked "does anybody know who that bouncing ball on legs was, last night, did you all see him? Stripy little fellow, blue, big feet?"

Hyssop mumbled something about bad dancing. Enoch guiltily sank deeper into his pool until only the tip of his trunk was showing, like a snorkel above the suds.

Did he know something they didn't?

Meanwhile, back at the Sodaslope laboratory, Doc Hibbert was beside himself with excitement. "Oh, Sudsy-doodles and Soapy-Poodles! We've got it Arthur, we're ready! Hold the ropes my dear lad … we could lose it now so easily, do you see how eager the spacebubbleship is to fly!"

Preparations had gone well. The bubbleship had gone through a series of thorough tests. It had been blown through a tunnel at high-velocity, pummeled with fluff balls and submerged under water. After a few minor alterations, the spacecraft had passed each test with flying colours.

The bubble wall was quivering with readiness.

"I can see it really wants to go now! It's time to call on the Bunnies!" said Arthur.

The Bunnies are expert flyers, they carry messages that are too important to get lost in a bubble call. By stretching themselves out and letting their large ears catch the wind they glide easily through the thin air. They brave windstorms and hurricanes, hard bubbles and soft bubbles, clouds of poisonous bubbles and hot burning bubbles, in order to deliver the post.

They come across bubbles that other Filzkins could never even dream of; fragile pearly bubbles, constantly changing colour, reflecting light from the rainbows that they fly through.

Graceful and serene creatures, the Bunnies are very much at home in the skies. They fly out over valleys and hills, soaring high above the clouds, until they are barely visible.

The Filzkin crew were still splashing around in the hot springs when the Bunnies flew in. They knew at once that they were bringing important news. Speaking softly the Bunnies made their announcement.

"Doc Hibbert has sent us here to let you all know that the spacebubbleship is ready to launch. And, he will expect you at his laboratory in three whortles time."

There was a noisy cheer from the crew. This was the message they had been waiting for.

And below ground, in his hole, Boris awoke with a start.

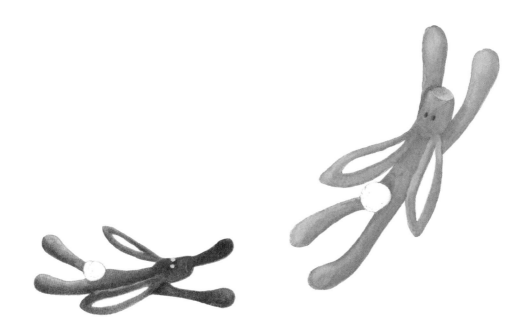

CHAPTER 10

The Big Day

Those 3 whortles passed very quickly for Mr. McKarr.

On the first whortle he began to pack his bag. As he was trying to decide which scarf would go with what mittens, he noticed Edgar's portrait on the wall, looking down at him.

"We're on our way Edgar. We'll bring you back safely!" he promised, earnestly.

On the second whortle, he cleaned his house from top to bottom, there is nothing worse for a Filzkin than to come back to a messy home.

Finally, on the third whortle, he set off up the hill with his bundle under his arm hoping to find the same speedy little slurch waiting for him.

He soon arrived at the laboratory where the whole crew were gathered. There was such a hustle and bustle! Each Filzkin was allowed to bring on board one special thing of his very own. It could be anything at all, as long as it was small.

They had been warned, that if the bubbleship became too full, it would wobble uncontrollably.

They chose the most random items you could imagine. Nevin brought his portable Mount Sylvian, complete with built-in bubble maker, (lovely, but about as useful to their mission as a giant cactus!)

Hyssop had brought his bubble-bag so that he could sleep in comfort.

And Pink Dawg, brought a giant cactus!

"You can't be serious, Pink Dawg!" cried Doc Hibbert with dismay. "Are you trying to burst the bubbleship before we even set off?"

Pink Dawg sheepishly took his cactus away and returned with a sombrero.

Finally, each and every one of them and their belongings, were safely checked and stowed aboard ship.

As is customary on O'Sudds, whenever the Filzkins embark on a journey, one Filzkin or another, will break into song and soon they all join in. This time it was Beetroot who started to sing.

Oh, Planet, O'Sudds we are leaving

To see what's out there in space

Though the "Great Outside" is calling

We'll surely be back someday.

There's a world out there to explore

We'll find plants and creatures galore

We'll seek them and greet them

And maybe we'll teach them

Of life on O'Sudds, and more!

Everyone sang the same words but to a different tune, (you should try this sometime).

Finally, the moment came for the spacebubbleship, with its motley crew of Filzkins, to be released into space.

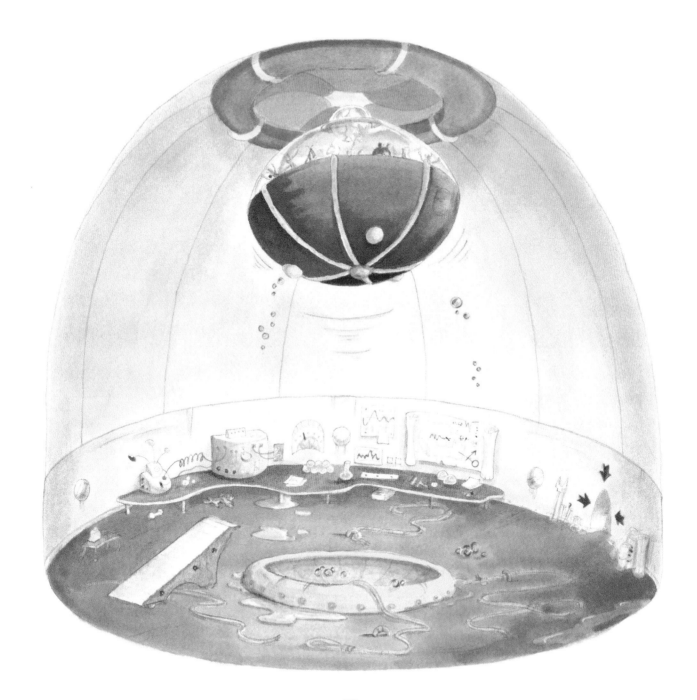

CHAPTER 11

Lift-off

Off it went! The bubbleship rose, slowly but surely off the ground, in absolute silence.

It wobbled and jiggled gently as the ropes fell away, and it was free. In the meantime the domed roof of the lab had begun to open. By the time the bubbleship had reached the roof, the opening to the sky was as wide as it would get.

Doc Hibbert was a live-wire of activity; darting about the controls pressing buttons here, pulling leavers there, plugging and unplugging, connecting and disconnecting. The crew looked on in disbelief, they had never seen him move so fast. He was checking monitors, comparing data and shouting commands that made no sense to any of the others.

Suddenly there was a deep "BOING"! And the bubbleship shuddered to halt. They all felt it. The entire crew were thrown upwards with the pressure of the bubbleship being squashed up against the opening of the roof. They fell back down only to be thrown up again and back down again with another "BOING"!

And so the bouncing went on until they finally stopped completely and all was still.

Oh dear! The spacebubbleship was stuck!

It was, in fact, too big to fit through the hole in the roof. Doc Hibbert was beside himself. "I can't understand how my calculations could be so wrong!"

Lost for words, the entire crew of Filzkins looked upwards in silence.

All that could be heard was the piercing squeak of the bubbleship trying to squeeze it's wiggly wobbly form out through the hole. It was painful to hear their beautiful new vessel creaking and groaning, as it twisted like a balloon being pinched and knotted into a sausage poodle.

"Doc..." said Arthur "...why don't you...".

But before Arthur could finish his sentence there was an almighty explosion followed by a loud "FOMP"!

They all thought that the ship had burst and expected to find themselves splattered all over the walls of the laboratory. Was it all over before their journey had even begun?

But no, the tough little bubbleship had in fact made it. It had blumped through the hole in the roof of the lab causing the Filzkins inside it to be tossed around like popcorn in a pan. What a hullaballoo!

When at last he was able to speak, Enoch apologized for his sneezing, explaining that some dust had got into his sensitive snout and there was nothing he could do about it. They all laughed as they realized that the almighty explosion had in fact been Enoch's gigantic sneeze! And it was this that had forced them through the roof! What a relief!

Free and in the open sky above the city, the spacebubbleship wobbled and wibbled out of shape for some time, until at length, it found its comfortable form again. A little shaken but relieved to be on their way, the Filzkins went back to their stations to pursue their duties. Their expedition to explore the cosmos and, hopefully, to rescue their friend Edgar, had begun.

Soon they had risen high enough to be able to spot famous landmarks on their planet. They were amazed to be able to see down into the belly of the crater of Soap Mount Sylvian. Through the scattered clouds of bubbles, they recognised the vast, soap-dust desert of the Yellowlands.

Meanwhile, Doc Hibbert was far away in his own world of numbers and calculations, his claw foot scribbling frantically on a notebook.

"Is something wrong?" said Mr. McKarr "you look worried".

"Well Mr. McKarr, there is a slight problem, but I'm working on it" said Doc Hibbert.

"Problem? What problem, Doc ? We made it through the roof, didn't we?"

"Yes, but only with the help of Enoch's sneeze! We should never have got stuck in the first place. As you well know I designed this ship to fit easily through the roof. The volume of all its contents decides its size. That includes everything that we checked on to the ship, including each one of us."

"Oh … I see…" said Mr. McKarr, beginning to understand.

"So, are you saying that perhaps someone has smuggled something extra onto the ship, Doc, making it bigger than it should be?"

"Exactly! But let's keep it between ourselves for now Mr. McKarr, we don't want to cause a panic on board, do we? Keep a look-out and let me know if you see or hear anything suspicious."

"Of course, Doc, of course" said Mr. McKarr, "you can count on me!"

Taking the controls once again, Doc Hibbert pulled on a big leaver and pressed two large buttons on his panel, causing the bubbleship to accelerate taking them higher and deeper into interstellar space, stretching slightly as it went.

Mr. McKarr felt honoured that Doc had confided in him, nevertheless, it made him very nervous.

As he turned away, something caught his eye, a glimmer, two little red lights in the shadow below the console. "Pull yourself together McKarr," he told himself, "you are beginning to imagine things now."

Pulling himself together, he joined the others as they watched O'Sudds shrink faster and faster from their view, until their home planet became a mere speck in the far distance.

Aliens!

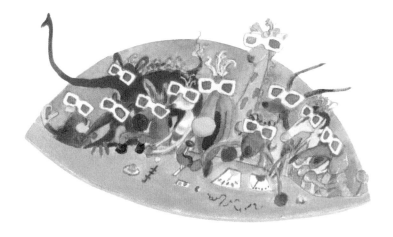

CHAPTER 12

Aliens!

Travelling at the speed of light, they soon found themselves out in the universe, steering away from their own galaxy with its floating bubbles, soap flakes and tumbling bundles of fluff.

They floated on through other planetary systems where their little bubbleship was challenged beyond all expectations. Sometimes the ship was blown about by cosmic turbulence and at other times squashed by magnetic fields into shapes that brought it dangerously close to bursting.

Each Filzkin had his own particular job to do and by and large they kept to them. But sometimes it was hard not to stare out into the void at the wonders outside their capsule, the view was truly captivating.

They could see planets shaped like eggs, that were growing and multiplying as they flew past them. There were planets that were totally flat like pancakes, these were especially dangerous as you could easily fly into them due to their being virtually invisible from certain angles. Other planets glowed with fluorescent light, to look at these they had to wear special glasses!

There was one very important duty that everyone was expected to do and that was, to watch over the LFD counter. The "Living Fluff Detector".

"Finding Edgar, will be like finding a needle in a haystack!" Doc Hibbert had told them at the start of the journey. "As you know there is a lot of fluff out there in the universe but this detector will identify *living* fluff and that, as we all know, is what we Filzkins are made of."

After travelling for several allors they found themselves in a Galaxy that looked strangely familiar.

"Doc, look! Bubbles and soap flakes!" said Zebbs excitedly.

"Oh yes!" shouted Hyssop.

"And I can see a planet … with two Suns! Just like ours!" called Muli in amazement.

Puzzled, they all turned and looked to Doc Hibbert for answers.

But before he could explain anything, there was a loud BANG! Something hit their bubbleship with such force that the lights flickered and the entire ship began to spin wildly on the spot. The red light of the Living Fluff Detector was flashing to the high pitched beeps of its alarm!

When the bubbleship finally stopped spinning, the whole crew were lying on the floor, dizzy and seeing stars! When they were able to focus again, they looked up to see an enormous face with big goggly eyes floating menacingly above them.

They were all terrified. What was it?

It was all too much for Otto. He scuttled into the darkness under the control panel for safety.

But almost immediately he sprang out again, shouting

"ALIENS!"

"They're on board! Under there!" he yelled, pointing to the console.

The entire crew were on the alert now and the air was charged with their collective fear. The alarm continued to beep frantically as they all turned to look toward the console. Was there an alien hiding there? And what was the strange looking thing outside their ship that seemed to be observing them with those enormous eyes?

At last the alarm stopped beeping and little Moley stepped forward towards the console. He cleared his throat and firmly announced "to any alienth who might be inthide or out-thide the thip, I'm Moley, third in command to Captain Doc Hibbert of the Cornithe Thellwell Thpathe-bubble-thip, we are on a peatheful mithon. We mean no harm to you or any life-formth. Pleathe communicate with uth!"

The others looked at Moley with renewed respect, they had never realised that he was so brave.

Slowly but surely a small, blue ringed creature, with sparkling red eyes, crawled nervously from the shadows under the console with his tail between his legs.

"I can't believe it! What on the Froth of Great Mount Sylvian are you doing here, Boris?" cried Enoch in amazement poking Boris with his long snout "...you should be at home with your family!"

"I … I just wanted to be part of your adventure uncle Enoch!" he replied.

Enoch looked at the little stowaway sternly. "How on *O'Sudds* did you get on board?"

Quaking from the tip of his horn to his big slipper feet, Boris replied sheepishly "I sneaked under Nielson's bathtub while you were all busy, didn' I."

"WHAT? Nielson, bathtub?" cried Doc Hibbert, suddenly realising what had made his spaceship unstable.

"And, by the way, that's Edgar out there! Can't you see?" continued Boris, pointing defiantly with his soft clamp paw.

"Woof, it *is* Edgar!" Barked Pink Dawg from the viewing cupola above.

Everyone looked towards the window. They watched as Edgar blinked once and slowly turned around. Little by little they began to make out the familiar shape of their missing friend, as he dangled listlessly from his bubble-head.

They were overjoyed and began clapping and cheering and hugging each other.

"Well, what are we waiting for, let's get him on board!" cried Mr. McKarr.

"Hold your horses! Not so fast!" said Doc Hibbert surprising them all.

"We can't possibly take another *thing* on board this ship! You have no idea how dangerously close we have come to bursting already!"

"Another "THING"? ...But that's our Edgar your talking about!" protested Zebbs.

"...that is, not until a certain *someone* reveals what has been brought on board this ship, that absolutely shouldn't have!" continued Doc Hibbert, looking straight at Nielson. "I think Nielson has something to tell us."

"Yes, well I've erm ... had a thought, I've decided, that for the benefit of our mission, to sacrifice a small item I may have erm, brought on board with me!" Nielson said, delicately placing his soft fluffy hooves together, "my, erm bathtub."

The crew listened in disbelief!

"Well, we'd better get a move on Nielson!" said Mr. McKarr beginning to climb down into the hold, "there's no time to lose."

They made a lot of noise and clatter down below in the hold. "I don't believe it!" Mr. McKarr could be heard muttering, "of all the items to have brought on board, Nielson! REALLY? A bathtub?"

The other Filzkins looked at each other and rolled their eyes as if to say "Nielson, what is he like?"

CHAPTER 13

Edgar's Rescue

Nevin cupped his woolly spoon hands on his head in utter exasperation. "Ok, that's it! I'm going to put my bubble-head on. Someone has to bring poor Edgar on board!"

Mr. McKarr turned to Doc Hibbert. "One big thing out and one small Edgar in, should be ok, right Doc?"

"Yes" said Doc Hibbert, "Nielson's tub *must* go out before Edgar can get in, it's simple mathematics!"

Soon Nevin and Mr. McKarr, fully prepared with bubble-heads on, were holding on to Nielson's bathtub and standing at the open air-lock ready to take their first leap out into the universe. They hesitated and their knees wobbled.

Even though they had practiced using their bubble-heads, this would still be the first time they would use them for real. They held their breath and closed their eyes before getting ready to jump.

It may have been one small step for a Filzkin but it was a giant leap for Filzkin-kind!

"Three, two, one!"

Pulling the bathtub behind them, they jumped. There was no turning back.

It was quite a spectacle! The Filzkins left on board were gripped by the scene.

There they were, Mr. McKarr and Nevin floating outside in space holding on to Nielson's large, white bath, slowly tumbling as if in a strange waltz as they tried to move it as far away from the ship as possible.

Not too far away, they could see Edgar, still floating limply, too exhausted to move.

Finally, thinking that they had left the tub safely behind them, Nevin and Mr. McKarr began to make their way towards Edgar. It looked as though they were swimming in mid-air. It was a very slow process and a frustrating one to watch.

Then, just as they were close enough for Mr. McKarr to reach out with his claw hand to take hold of Edgar's drumstick paw, in this tense celestial moment, he was pulled away with a sharp tug.

His foot had got tangled up in the chain of the bath plug!

The others watched in horror as he was pulled slowly down underneath their ship. He mouthed a silent scream of anguish "Oh ... NOOooo!"

They say, that in space, no one can hear you scream...

There was nothing that Nevin could do to help him, right now, he had to be brave and concentrate on rescuing Edgar.

After further space-paddling with his spoon hands, he managed at last to reach Edgar. The crew watched him carefully tie his tail around Edgar's paw and start to space-swim back to the air-lock, pulling the limp Edgar behind him.

Meanwhile, Mr. McKarr, had managed to grab hold of the door to the air-lock but the unwieldy tub was still pulling dangerously at his foot.

Nevin now had to free Mr. McKarr from the chain, with Edgar still attached to his tail!

It was not easy, but eventually, Nevin managed to disentangle Mr. McKarr from the chain and Neilson's excess baggage was released. The tub drifted away from the ship, turning first on its side and then upside-down, making slow-motion summersaults as it went.

The three exhausted friends clambered on board to loud cheering. They were happy, Edgar was safely on board and their very first space walk had been a success!

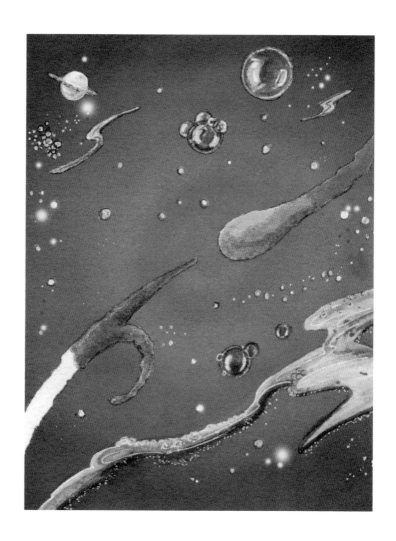

CHAPTER 14

Crank Up the Engine

After ditching the bathtub, there was a noticeable change, the spacebubbleship immediately stabilised and stopped wobbling and quivering.

"...It's ok, you know," announced Nielson magnanimously, "you don't have to thank me, one has to make sacrifices sometimes for the greater good!"

They all laughed and shook their heads. It didn't matter anymore, Edgar had been rescued and all were safely on board.

Enjoying a bowl of marshmallow pudding and a cup of frothy tea, while chatting to his friends, Edgar was slowly getting back to his old self.

"You were right all along," he said, turning to Mr. McKarr, "I should have waited to join the rest of you. Now, I see how silly I was. Goodness knows what might have happened if you hand't come to my rescue."
"There *is* strength in numbers, you see Edgar!" said Pablo with his usual wisdom.

"And we aren't here *just* to rescue you, Edgar, we have a whole expedition ahead of us!" said Mr. McKarr, "and this time we're all going together."

Back at his console, Doc Hibbert was looking a bit embarrassed. "Umm er ... listen everyone, I have er um ... something rather important to tell you. That big planet you see over there is um er ... in fact O'Sudds!"

"How's that Doc?" asked Arthur, very surprised.

"It seems that we've been flying in circles until now, because of that bathtub!" explained Doc. "...we've come all the way back to our very own galaxy."

Soon, sure enough, they were able to spot the twin suns disappearing behind O'Sudds, to be replaced by the familiar glow of the Motherlight in the distance.

However, even though their beloved planet was within easy reach and did look very welcoming, none of them wanted to go home just yet.

They all wanted to continue on their expedition.

Only one question remained, which direction should they take?

It was an easy decision to make. They were all drawn to a bright cloud of glowing stars. From far away, at the very end of the universe. It seemed to be calling to them with a kind of magic.

Doc ordered everyone to return to their stations.

"Crank up the engine Arthur!" he said.

Arthur turned a few dials and pulled a big lever causing the spacebubbleship to make a swift turn and surge forward eagerly. As it began to accelerate towards its new destination, it let off a stream of healthy, plump bubbles in it's wake.

What they would find at the end of their journey, none of them knew.

Soon, they were floating away, leaving Nielson's bathtub turning and tumbling, alone in the darkness.

The End ... to be continued...

The Official Crew List of the Cornice Thellwell Spacebubbleship

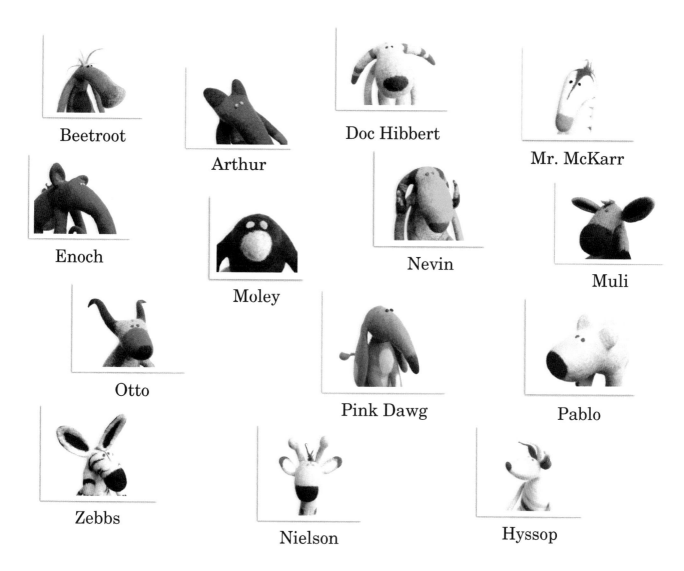

Beetroot

Arthur

Doc Hibbert

Mr. McKarr

Enoch

Moley

Nevin

Muli

Otto

Pink Dawg

Pablo

Zebbs

Nielson

Hyssop

All you need to know about O'Sudds
...but were too afraid to ask

Units and measurements

- 1 Milworth = about a year and 6 months on Earth

- 1 Ollard = approximately 3 of our Earth days

- 1 Whortle is nearly half a day

- 1 Allor = 0.8 hours (1 Allor is made up of 32 Roodles and Roodles are made up of 17 Imps, are you any the wiser?)

- 1 Tickle = 803 km

- 1 Padoliter is approximately the length of 10 Filzkins with outstretched arms standing in a row. (about 7.5 Metres)

- 1 Barolitor = half a swimming pool of liquid

- 1 Ronald = 37.8 Metres

- Darlings are the Currency on O'Sudds (exchange rate may change by the allor)

Appliances on O'Sudds

- Slurch: available for free, an individual capsule that can be picked up wherever one is to be found.

- Bubblestream: like a telephone but more complex and advanced, as well as messages it is even able to carry smells encapsulated in a bubble.

- The Pan-Kalang: a large musical instrument offering something for everyone to play.

- LFD: a "Living Fluff Detector" a gadget that can detect any fluff with life in it e.g. a Filzkin.

Seasons

There are only two seasons on O'Sudds:

- Bubblefall when it rains bubbles

- Fluffdown when fluff falls from above

Provinces and Islands on O'Sudds

- Foamapoama, Sylvian, Alkalina, Graceland, Seifen, The Hardlands, Crumble, Yellowlands, Isla Sapona, Island of Slip, Luxo (The Flaky Plains of...)

Oceans, Seas, Lakes & Rivers

- Medisapona sea
- The Great Soak is the northern ocean
- The Great Melt is the southern ocean
- Lake Awa located between the Province of Crumble and the Flaky Plains of Luxo
- River Babala Nadi has it's origin at Lake Awa
- River Wash is the longest river on O'Sudds

Cities, Towns and other places of interest

- Washingtown City is in the Province of Foamapoama
- Sodaslope University: Doc Hibbert's laboratory is in the town of Washingtown City
- Saponaville is Mr. McKarr's home town in the Province of Graceland east of the Bongbón Hills
- Bubble reach Mountains situated in the Foamapoama Province
- Slippery: Arthur's home town, a large town in the Alkalina Province
- Frothley forest in the Alkalina Province where Otto lives

- The Weightless Caves are in the Bubble Reach Mountains of Foamapoama

- Soap Mount Sylvian is a giant soapcano on O'Sudds and is about 1,300 padolitors high

- Hot Bubble Springs near Soap Mount Sylvian

- Isla Sapona is Nielson's floating island

- Pooder - where Moley lives

- Wallowbath - where Boris lives

- Soap on the Water - Muli and Pink Dawg live there

- Aleppo is where Zebbs lives

- Duft is the city where Enoch is at home

- Glide is where Pablo lives

- City of Treswigod on the Island of Slip, Hyssop comes from there

- Bröckelstadt is in the Province of Crumble, where Edgar comes from

- Savon D'or on the river Wash in the province of Sylvian where Beetroot lives

- The Schaumberg Hills are in the Yellowlands where Nevin lives

Meet The FILZKINS®

Mr. McKarr is well-meaning and helpful, if a little nosey. He can't resist a new gadget or the chance of an adventure. He never doubts his own abilities and thinks he can do absolutely anything.

Doc Hibbert is a scientist and a real brainbox. He spends most of his time at his laboratory attempting to build the perfect spacebubbleship. His busy mind is always occupied with trying to solve difficult mathematical problems and making scientific discoveries.

Hyssop is a bit of a drama queen, he tends to think the world revolves around him and gets a bit moody when he doesn't get his own way. He loves spending time at the local Observatory looking at the stars. He's brilliant at picking up new languages.

Pablo is the big thinker. Other Filzkins come to him for advice. Wise and considerate he always has a little saying ready to use. He's often found sitting quietly, looking up at the sky, just thinking.

Otto is shy and a little nervous he is easily startled. Being a forest creature, he is often seen dashing away and hiding at the first hint of danger. He can run faster than any other Filzkin.

Enoch is a large and avuncular Filzkin. He is lovable and dependable, one can always rely on him. But, poor Enoch is burdened by the Planet's most sensitive nose! The tiniest puff of dust, makes him sneeze like a volcano!

Pink Dawg is a bit of a dreamer. He adores being the centre of attention. He can sniff out scents, retrieve lost objects and dig holes at high speed. He often chooses to do what he *wants* to do rather than what he ought to.

Moley is a restless little Filzkin, always kept busy with something. He is a cool dude with a cute lisp. Moley passes his time burrowing for choice nuggets of soap with his magnifying glass or studying the flora, gathering information like a detective.

Muli is quite a strong little Filzkin and is able to carry 5 times his own weight, when you can get him to do it. He can be a little stubborn at times, not always willing to do what others want, sometimes needing to be bribed with marshmallows.

Beetroot is so laid back he his almost horizontal. This gives him plenty of opportunity to study the stars. Music and water are his favourite things and he spends most of his lazy days playing on the Pan-Kalang. He is cool and relaxed and has a calming effect on other beings.

Boris is a bouncing ball on legs. He is a determined little Filzkin and always wants to be a part of everything. He has incredible acrobatic skills and enjoys bouncing and levitating in the air but he is equally as good at sliding along at high speed on his slipper feet.

Arthur is very inquisitive and always wants to know what's going on and why. He is the "fixer", miraculously finding exactly what is needed for fixing stuff. With that long snout of his he can sniff out any item likely to become useful at some later time, but don't ask him where he got it.

Zebbs likes to look strong and tough but he is in fact a thoughtful and gentle character with a keen sense of right and wrong. He will stand up for anyone who is wrongly treated and makes a great and loyal friend.

Nielson is elegant, dignified, suave and sophisticated and has excellent manners. He enjoys the luxuries of life and does it with style and good taste. Considered a little snooty by some he is well loved by all who know him, for his fun ways and wonderful sense of humour.

Edgar is pretty clever and can conjure up solutions when the rest of the group are puzzled. He is a bit like the chameleon, able to blend into the background. Unfortunately, his camouflage isn't always as convincing as he believes. He is from a long line of space explorers (see Cornice Thellwell) and is keen to follow in their footsteps.

Black & Yellow Bunny are sweet and innocent little Filzkins. They can fly by gliding, using their wing-like ears for many allors at a time, often carrying messages over long distances. However they need lots of sleep and can often nod off at the wrong moment if not in the air.

Nevin just zings with energy. He is so hyperactive, he just can't keep still! However he worries a lot too, walking around with lots of concerns in his head. He has a pair of spoon hands that can catch everything that flies in his direction and makes him a brilliant juggler.

Cornice Thellwell was Edgar's grandmother and had been somewhat of a space travel pioneer in her time, making several attempts (not always successful) to journey through space. The spacebubbleship is named in her honour.

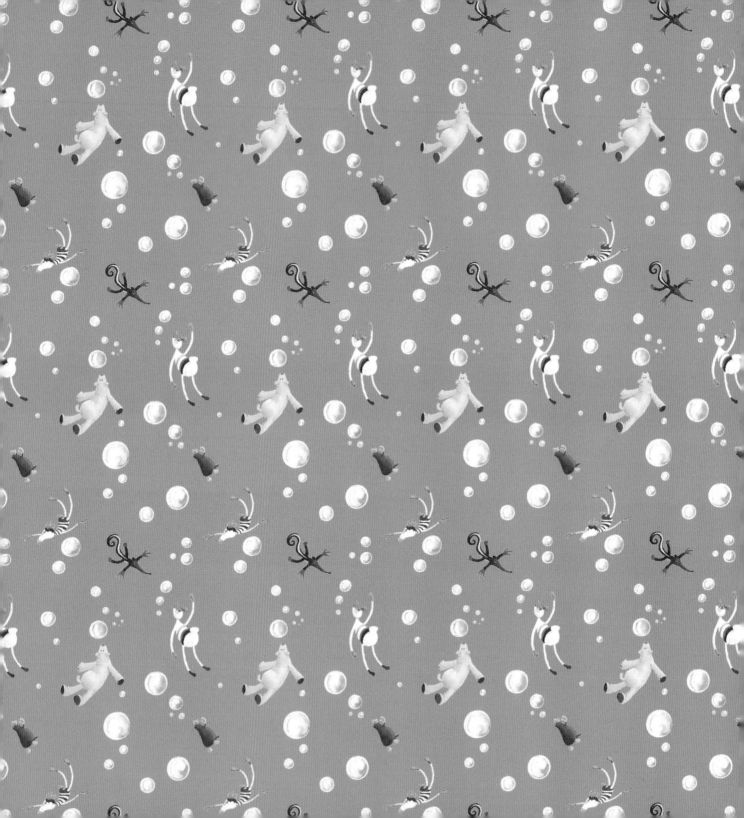

We hope you enjoyed reading about the
Filzkins and their adventures.

If you would like your own hand felted Filzkin
in merino wool you can get one from
www.seboldsoriginals.com
Have a look at our video to see how a Filzkin
is replicated here on Planet Earth.

23693006R00063

Printed in Poland
by Amazon Fulfillment
Poland Sp. z o.o., Wrocław